THE LEGEND OF DAVE THE VILLAGER 4

by Dave Villager

First Print Edition (August 2019)

BOOK FOUR:
The Cool Dude Battle Royale

The Legend of Dave the Villager 4

CHAPTER ONE

Cool Island

"This is another fine mess you've got me into," said Carl.

"I am sorry, chaps," said Porkins. "I need to know when to keep my mouth jolly well shut."

"How about *all* the time?" said Carl. "If it helps, I can sew your mouth shut for you. I'm very handy with a needle and thread."

"Don't be too hard on Porkins," said Dave. "I think they would have taken three prisoners whatever happened."

"Yes," said Carl, "but they might have taken three *different* prisoners. Not us!"

The three of them were locked up in jail cells in the bowels of the big ship. The villagers holding them prisoner called themselves the *Cool Dudes*.

The villager who seemed to be in charge, the one with the red baseball cap, had told Dave, Carl and Porkins that they were being entered into the *Cool Dude Battle Royale*

4

—a one-hundred man battle to the death on a place called "Cool Island."

Dave had never heard of the "Cool Dudes" before, or their "Battle Royale", but he knew it was something he wanted no part of.

"Just keep your wits about you," Dave said. "As soon as we get a chance, we make our escape."

Annoyingly, the villagers had taken his rucksack, so building a portal was out of the question. And they'd taken his weapons and armor too.

"I seem to spend most of my life getting captured these days," sighed Carl. "I think I'm actually getting used to it."

Suddenly the ship began to wobble, then it slowly came to a stop.

"We must be here," said Dave.

"Oh goody," said Carl. "How exciting."

A door opened and three villagers in baseball caps entered, accompanied by an iron golem.

"Come with us," one of the villagers said. "And don't try anything."

They led Dave, Carl and Porkins out of the door and down a corridor. Finally they reached a ladder.

"Climb," said the villager.

Dave, Carl and Porkins climbed, Dave leading the way. When he got to the top he opened a trapdoor, the daylight hurting his eyes. He climbed out onto the deck of the ship. When his eyes finally adjusted to the sight his mouth dropped open in shock.

The ship was docked in a harbor, but the harbor wasn't what Dave was staring at. Beyond the harbor was a city—the biggest city Dave had ever seen. Actually, Dave realized, it was the *only* city he'd ever seen. It was covered in towers made from a hundred different materials, all lit up by neon lights. There were diamond towers, emerald towers, even *sponge* towers. And in the middle of the city was a tower twice as large as the others, made of solid gold. On the side of the tower, made from flashing redstone lights, was the word *COOL*.

Porkins and Carl were on deck now, also looking in amazement at the city.

The villager in the red baseball cap appeared behind them.

"I didn't introduce myself earlier," he said. "I'm Ron, personal assistant to Derek Cool."

"Who the heck is Derek Cool?" said Carl.

"The mayor of this city," said Ron. "The guy in charge of everything you see before you. Welcome... to Cool Island."

CHAPTER TWO

Cool City

Dave wasn't surprised at all to hear that the city on Cool Island was called Cool City. As he, Porkins and Carl were led through the streets, he saw that life in Cool City seemed to be one long party. DJs were playing music on the street, people were dancing, and everyone seemed to be in a good mood.

The villagers who lived in the city wore all sorts of extravagant clothes of many different colors, and a lot of them wore sunglasses—even though it was night.

The guards leading Dave and the others through the city all wore baseball caps and sunglasses—that seemed to be their uniform.

"Hey," a villager with dyed green hair said as they passed, "are you three dudes entering the tournament this year?"

"Yes they are," said Ron, who was leading the guards.

"Right on!" said the villager. "Can't wait to see you on

TV!"

"So what's the deal with this tournament to the death thing?" Carl asked Ron.

"You'll find out more when we get to Cool Tower, creeper," said Ron.

As they got nearer to Cool Tower, most of the people in the streets wore clothing made of gold and emeralds. It didn't look very comfortable to Dave. The streets here were made of gold too—solid gold blocks.

"Where did all this gold come from?" Dave marveled. "I didn't know there was this much gold in the whole world!"

"Derek Cool's father was a brave explorer," said Ron. He came to this island years ago, without an emerald to his name, and discovered that the mountains were filled with gold. He set up a mine, made his fortune and built Gold City."

"Gold City?"

"That was what the city used to be called. But when Derek took over after his dad passed, he renamed it Cool City. He wanted it to be the coolest place on earth."

They finally reached Cool Tower. A villager in a bellboy outfit opened the door for them. As Dave walked into the lobby he was amazed to see that everything inside —from the front desk to the doors—was made of gold. The only thing that wasn't gold was the plush red carpet.

"Wow," said Carl. "Your mayor may be cool, but he doesn't have much taste."

"Silence!" snapped Ron. "Don't you dare talk about our mayor like that! You will keep a civil tongue when you meet Derek Cool, creeper, or you will pay for it later. Do I make myself clear?"

"Ok, ok," said Carl. "I was only joking."

"Oh yes," said Ron, "that's another thing. If the mayor makes a joke, you must laugh. Got it?"

"Even if it's not funny?" said Porkins.

"*Especially* if it's not funny!" said Ron. "I say this for your own sake. The mayor, for all his great qualities, is not exactly, um, keen on people disagreeing with him. Or not being nice to him. Or not laughing at his jokes. Oh, and if he asks you if he's cool—please, please please tell him he's cool."

"Is he not cool?" asked Carl.

Everyone in the lobby gasped. A waitress dropped a tray, glass shattering across the floor.

"The mayor is the coolest person who ever lived," Ron said nervously. "He is amazing and awesome and definitely—definitely, definitely, *definitely*—not a nerd. Got it?"

"Um, ok," said Carl.

He led Dave, Carl and Porkins towards an elevator. Dave was completely unsurprised to see that the elevator was made of gold too. Ron entered the elevator with them, leaving the baseball cap guards in the lobby.

"Remember," said Ron sternly as the elevator began to rise, "be on your best behavior." He adjusted his red baseball cap, making sure it was straight.

"So Derek Cool, the mayor, his father founded this city?" asked Carl.

"That's correct," said Ron.

"Was his name Cool as well?"

Ron bristled. "No," he said. "Derek changed his family name after his father passed away."

"So his real surname isn't *Cool?*"

"No," snapped Ron.

"So what was it originally?" Carl asked.

"Wimpy."

Carl snorted. "Derek Wimpy! No wonder he changed it."

Ron turned on Carl, fury in his eyes. "If I were you, little creeper, I would watch my tongue. The mayor *hates* his old surname, so make sure you never mention it in his presence."

"Alright," said Carl. "But one more thing: when you captured us you told us you were an ancient order of knights who have served the coolest dudes in history. Is that true, or just some lie that Derek told you to say?"

Ron's cheeks went red. "It is not a *lie*, creeper. We are

an order of knights. All of my Baseball Cap Boys are great warriors."

Carl laughed. "Baseball Cap Boys!" he said. "What a terrible name."

"Creeper!" Ron yelled. "The mayor himself gave us that name, so *watch your tongue!*"

"Aha!" said Carl. "So Derek set up your little group of knights. You're not an ancient order after all!"

Ron's face was bright red.

"Not technically," he said. "The... the mayor likes us to say that. He thinks it sounds... *cool.*"

Carl grinned. "The more I hear about this mayor of yours, the less cool he sounds."

"You try saying that to him," said Ron. "See what happens to you."

"Maybe I will," said Carl.

"Carl, calm down," said Dave. "Don't go causing any trouble."

"As if I would," said Carl.

PING!

The elevator came to a stop.

"We're here," said Ron. "Behave yourselves."

The elevator doors slid open.

CHAPTER THREE
Derek Cool

In front of Dave was a huge room. As far as he could tell, the room took up a whole floor of the tower, with windows looking out in every direction.

The carpet was a deep red and all the furniture was gold. A jukebox in the corner was playing some music. Dave could just about make out the lyrics:

Derek Cool, is the coolest of them all,

His teachers couldn't teach him, 'cus he's too cool for school.

If you don't recognize his brilliance then you are a fool,

Because he is the coolest, the coolest of them all!

Various cool-looking people were lounging around the room, playing video games, watching tv, or just lying on the furniture.

At the back of the room was a huge throne made of gold blocks, and on it sat the fattest villager Dave had ever seen. He was wearing a white baseball cap, sunglasses, and a golden tracksuit. And he was munching on a cooked chicken.

"Your coolness," Ron announced. "May I present the last three warriors for this year's tournament."

He pushed Dave, Carl and Porkins forward.

"Right on," said the fat villager. "Ron, I was worried you weren't gonna be able to get enough warriors this year."

"It was a bit of a struggle, but we managed it," said Ron. "Warriors, this is our mayor, Derek Cool. The coolest dude in the galaxy."

"That's right," said Derek. "No-one's cooler than me. Here, watch this!"

He staggered to his feet, then waddled over to the foot of the throne, where there was a red skateboard. Derek picked up the skateboard in his fat hand, then placed it on the ground.

"Are you sure this is wise, your coolness?" Ron asked.

Derek scowled. "What's the matter, Ron?" he said. "You don't think I'm *cool* enough to skateboard?"

"No, no, of course not," said Ron quickly.

"Good," said Derek. "Come on everyone!" he shouted. "Watch me do some awesome tricks!"

Everyone gathered round. From the bored looks on their faces, Dave guessed that this was the kind of thing

Derek did a lot: showing off how *cool* he was.

Derek Cool placed one foot on the skateboard. It groaned from the strain.

"I feel sorry for that skateboard," whispered Carl.

"Ssh," said Dave.

Derek gingerly used his other foot to push the board forward. It began to slowly roll across the floor, somehow managing to hold his weight.

"Well done, Mr Mayor!" someone yelled.

"Wow, such speed!" yelled another.

Derek was skateboarding so slowly that he was barely moving, but all the cool hangers on were cheering him on as if this was the most brilliant thing they'd ever seen.

"Yeah, look at me!" Derek yelled. "Tell me how cool I am!"

"You're so cool!" someone said.

Derek was so distracted by all the praise that he lost control, and the board began to roll across the room at speed.

"Waaaaaaa!!!!" yelled Derek.

CRASSSH!!! David smashed into a golden sofa. He ended up on his back and the skateboard broke in two.

All the cool hangers on cheered.

"That was amazing!" said one.

"That was the coolest thing I've ever seen!" said another.

Ron came over and helped Derek to his feet. Unlike everyone else in the room, Ron looked embarrassed.

"Did I do good, Ron?" Derek asked. "Am I cool?"

"Very cool, sir," said Ron.

"Yeah!" said Derek. "I'm cool, I'm cool!"

Dave, Porkins and Carl could only watch in amazement as everyone gathered around Derek, telling him how cool he was.

"I say," said Porkins, "I hate to be harsh, but he acts like a big baby. He's a fully grown man!"

"He's a spoiled brat," said Carl. "Because he's rich, everyone tells him what he wants to hear."

Carl had it right, Dave thought. From the looks of things, Derek Cool had been surrounded by people telling him what he wanted to hear his entire life.

"What about you three?" Derek said, waddling over to them. "Did you think I looked cool?"

Dave gave Carl a nudge.

"Oh, sooooo cool," said Carl. "I once went to a snow biome and I thought *that* was cool, but you're even cooler."

"What about you, piggy?" Derek said to Porkins.

"It was, er, a spiffing display," said Porkins. "Really top draw stuff."

"I agree," said Dave, "it was amazing."

Dave was tempted to tell Derek he'd looked like an idiot, but he knew it would only lead to trouble. He, Carl and Porkins had to keep their heads down for now and stay out of trouble, until they could figure out a way to escape.

"So you're warriors," said Derek. He looked down at Carl, who was half the size of a regular creeper. "You don't look much like warriors."

"Oh we are, your coolness," said Dave. "We're seasoned warriors. We've fought zombies, zombie pigmen, endermen, robots, all sorts."

"Don't forget the Kraken," said Carl.

"Oh yes," said Dave. "We defeated a kraken as well."

"Well you're about to face your greatest battle," Derek said, wiping the flecks of chicken from his mouth with his sleeve. "My tournament is the greatest tournament in the history of the world. Isn't that right, everyone?"

"Oh yes," all the hangers on replies. "It's so great!"

"Come with me, warriors," Derek said. He walked over to one side of the room and Dave, Carl and Porkins followed.

Derek brought them over to the windows that overlooked the city. The view up here was incredible, Dave thought. Cool Tower was so high that they could see the entire city stretching out before them; all the colorful towers made from different blocks. Far in the distance he could see the docks, which were filled with luxury ships, their white hulls glistening in the moonlight. The wooden ship that had brought them was there too.

"This whole city is mine," said Derek. "This is what you get for working hard. No-one ever gave me anything. I worked for every emerald that I have."

"I thought your father founded the city?" said Carl.

"I earned everything I have!" Derek snapped. "I renamed the city *Cool City*—that was all me!"

"Wow," said Carl. "You renamed a city. What a hero."

"Thanks!" said Derek, completely missing Carl's sarcasm. "The people in this city are all my best friends, they all love me. And one of the reasons they love me is because every year I put on the greatest tournament the world has ever seen!"

He waddled over to the other side of the room, Dave and the others following him. When they got there, Dave's mouth dropped open in shock.

Stretching out into the distance was the rest of the island. There was no city on this side of the island, just a mishmash of different biomes: snow, mountains, desert and more. But that wasn't what Dave had been so shocked by. What shocked him was that all these biomes were surrounded by a wall. A wall so high that it was almost as tall as Cool Tower. The wall had separated out a huge square of the island, sealing it in.

"That's the arena," Derek said excitedly. "One-hundred warriors go in, and only one comes out. It's a

Battle Royale!"

Dave was amazed at the size of the arena. But he was starting to get scared too. *Once we're trapped in there, there's no way out,* he thought. The wall seemed to be made of iron blocks, and there were guard towers along the top at regular intervals.

"So, one-hundred people all fight to the *death?*" said Carl. Even he sounded a bit worried.

"That's right!" said Derek. "We'll be filming you the whole time. It's the most popular TV show in Cool City, and *I* invented it!"

"What does the winner get?" asked Carl. "I mean, apart from the opportunity to not be dead."

Derek's face went serious. "The winner," he said, "gets a prize that money can't buy. Something so spectacular that it's hard to put into words. They get... a solid gold house!!!"

He pointed to a hilltop in the distance, on the edge of the city. On it were rows of golden houses.

"That's Winners Row," said Derek, "the most exclusive neighborhood in Cool City. Only tournament winners are allowed to live there. If you win, that'll be your new home."

"Listen," said Carl, "as great as a solid gold house sounds, I'm not sure me and my friends can take part in your tournament any more. I've had a bit of a cold recently, and I think Dave's coming down with something too. And just look at Porkins—his cheeks are blushing pink. Maybe you should find three other warriors."

"Ron," said Derek, fury in his eyes, "you said these were my last three warriors!"

"They... they are, your coolness," said Ron. "They all want to take part, I promise you. The creeper is only making a joke."

"I'm really not," said Carl.

"You sure he's joking?" Derek asked.

"Yes, your coolness," said Ron.

"Ha, good joke, creeper!" said Derek. He waddled back over and sat down on his throne. "What are your names, warriors? You first, creeper."

"I'm Carl," said Carl.

"Is that it?" snapped Derek. "You're not going to tell me what a spectacular warrior you are, and how you are honored to fight and die for me?"

"O-k," said Carl. "I'm Clubber Carl, the mightiest creeper who ever lived. Other creepers fear my name."

And...?" said Derek.

"Oh, and it's a great honor to fight and die for you... your coolness."

Dave could see from Carl's face that the creeper was doing everything he could to stop himself from making a sarcastic comment.

"You next, villager," said Derek.

"Um, I'm Dave the Destroyer," said Dave. "I'm so tough that I eat an enderman for breakfast and a zombie for lunch."

"What about dinner?" one of the cool hangers on asked.

"Just a mushroom stew," said Dave. "I, er, love to fight, and I'll be honored to fight in this tournament for you, Mayor Cool."

"Good, good," said Derek, taking a cooked chicken from a platter a servant was holding and starting to eat it. "And die for me, if need be?"

"Oh, I'd love to," said Dave.

"Your turn, pigman," said Derek, mouth full of chicken.

"I am Porkins the Magnificent!" said Porkins. "The last of the pigmen and destroyer of rotters and scoundrels everywhere! And it would be an honor to fight and die for you, sire."

"*Sire,* I like that," grinned Derek. "Good, good, you three really are a trio of cool dudes. I can't wait to see you on TV tomorrow. Ron, take them to the warriors enclosure!"

"Come on you three," said Ron, leading them to the elevator. "You need to get some sleep. You've got a big day ahead of you tomorrow."

They got into the elevator, the doors closing behind

them. It was just Dave, Carl, Porkins and Ron. As the elevator began to move down, Dave looked over at Carl and Porkins and saw that they were thinking the same thing as him:

This might be our last chance to escape.

Their weapons had all been confiscated, along with the rest of their belongings. Ron's sword hung in the scabbard on his belt, but he was busy paying attention to the numbers on the digital display as they went down.

It was now or never...

Dave gave Carl and Porkins a nod, and the three of them leapt forward, grabbing Ron.

"Unhand me!" he yelled.

"Carl, get his sword!" said Dave. The creeper slid round, pulling Ron's sword from the scabbard with his mouth, then chucking it to Dave. Dave caught it and pointed the blade at Ron.

"Don't move," said Dave.

Ron snarled, but he stayed still.

"Well done, chaps!" said Porkins. "We ruddy well did it!"

PING!

The elevator door opened. A huge gang of baseball cap wearing Cool Dudes were waiting for them, all of them holding swords.

"Oh crumbs," said Porkins.

21

CHAPTER FOUR

The Opening Ceremony

The Cool Dudes brought Dave, Carl and Porkins to a building next to the wall. As they approached the wall from below, Dave was once again staggered at how tall it was. The building looked like a little toy next to it, but as they got nearer Dave saw that the building was huge too: just nowhere near as huge as the wall. It was a dull building made of iron blocks, surrounded by wooden watchtowers, where Cool Dudes stood guard.

"This is the Warriors Enclosure," Ron told them. "This is where you'll stay until the opening ceremony tomorrow. And don't even *think* about trying to escape—we've got guards everywhere."

"We would never dream of it," said Carl.

"You think you're funny, don't you, creeper?" snapped Ron. "But you won't be laughing tomorrow. You're gonna be all alone in the arena, with ninety-nine other people trying to get you. How long do you think you'll last? I've got a bet on with the boys that you won't even last an hour."

"Then I'll do my best to make sure I die as quickly as possible," said Carl. "I'd hate to think of you losing a bet because of me. Judging by your clothes, you could do with all the money you can get."

"Just keep joking, creeper," said Ron. "I can't wait to see you on TV tomorrow."

Inside the building they were led down a corridor full of identical steel doors. Each door had a small window, and every so often Dave would see a face at a window as they passed. Most were villagers, but Dave occasionally saw a zombie or a skeleton, or other mobs he didn't recognize. The doors had numbers on them as well. Finally they reached the end of the corridor, where there were three open doors. The numbers on these were 98, 99 and 100.

"Get in," Ron told them.

"Can't we share a cell?" Porkins asked.

"No," said Ron. "The next time you three meet, it'll be in the arena." He grinned nastily. "Good luck—especially you, creeper."

This is it, thought Dave, *the very last chance to escape.* He swiveled round and tried to grab Ron's sword, but Ron was too quick, dodging backwards out of the way.

One of the guards pulled a weapon from his belt. It

looked like a redstone torch to Dave, but the tip was blue instead of red. The villager thrust it forward into Dave's stomach, and he was zapped with electricity.

"Dave!" Porkins yelled.

Dave staggered backwards in a daze. The guards roughly pushed him into a cell, then slammed the door shut. Ron appeared at the glass, smiling at him.

Ron and the guards left. Dave ran to the door to try and open it, but it was locked tight. Across the corridor he could see Carl and Porkins, looking back at him through the windows of their own cells.

He smiled at Carl and Porkins, to try and assure them that everything was alright, but the doors were soundproofed, so they couldn't speak to each other. Eventually Dave went over and slumped down on the bed in the corner of his cell. The only other things in the room were a toilet and a screen on the wall—although the screen had no buttons and there was no remote, so Dave had no way of turning it on. There was also a strange round pad on the floor made of a shiny material that Dave didn't recognize.

It was a tricky situation, but Dave still had hope that he, Carl and Porkins could escape. *They still have to bring us to the arena,* he thought. *When they let us out of our cells, we'll have to try to break free again.*

As he lay down on the bed he started to wonder about

the other 'warriors' competing in the tournament. Were they all taking part against their will, like him, Porkins and Carl, or had they volunteered?

Despite all his worries, Dave soon found himself drifting off to sleep. He dreamed of home, remembering his soft bed and his mother's cooking.

BWWAARRRMM!!!

Dave was woken by an alarm, coming from a speaker in the room's ceiling.

"Rise and shine, warriors," said Ron's voice over the speaker. "Breakfast time."

A few moments later a hatch opened in the bottom of Dave's door, and a plate with two eggs on it came through.

Dave greedily wolfed down the eggs. Then, to his surprise, the TV screen turned on.

"Welcome ladies and gentlemen," said an announcer on the TV, "to the fifth annual Cool Dude Battle Royale!"

Dave sat on his bed and watched the screen. A huge crowd was gathered around Cool Tower, everyone cheering and waving.

Then the footage switched to a balcony on the tower. Derek Cool stepped out onto it and the crowd went wild.

"Here's our magnificent leader," the announcer continued, "the coolest dude of them all... DEREK COOL!!!"

The crowd went crazy: people were whistling and

cheering and throwing their hats in the air.

"DEREK!" the crowd chanted. "DEREK! DEREK! DEREK!"

Derek waved at the crowd, soaking up the applause.

I'd love to biff that smug face of his, thought Dave bitterly. *Biff him right on the nose!*

Derek put his hands up and the crowd fell silent.

"Yo yo yo!" he shouted. The crowd cheered.

"We love you Derek!" someone shouted.

"Welcome to the fifth Cool Dude Battle Royale!" said Derek. "Every year I let the greatest warriors on the planet duke it out, to see who is the World's Coolest Warrior!"

The crowd all cheered and whooped.

"As always, we've got one-hundred brave warriors," continued Derek, "all competing for the most coveted award on Cool Island... a solid gold house!"

"Oooo!" said the crowd.

"So without further ado," said Derek, "let the tournament begin!"

Suddenly a hissing noise came from the floor. Dave jumped in shock, thinking it must be a creeper, but then he saw it was the round panel. It was pulsating with light and making strange noises.

"*Step onto the pad,*" said a robotic voice.

Dave looked at the pad, which was now sending up blasts of white smoke, the white light pulsating like a heartbeat.

"Er, no," said Dave. "I don't think I will."

"*Step onto the pad,*" repeated the voice. Then purple smoke starting pouring out of an air vent in the ceiling.

"*Poison gas is entering the room,*" said the robotic voice. "*Step onto the pad please. Step onto the pad or you will die.*"

Dave began to cough. The purple gas was filling his lungs, making it hard to breathe.

Looks like I don't have much choice, he thought, staggering towards the bright light of the pad. He stepped onto it.

FLOOSH!!!

There was a brief flash of white light, then Dave wasn't standing in his cell anymore—he was in the middle of a large, open grassy field. He could see mountains in the distance, and, beyond them, a huge wall.

Oh god, he thought, *I've teleported inside the arena!*

"Maggot!" a gruff voice roared. Dave turned and saw a huge villager, with muscles on his arms that were bigger than Dave's head.

"You have the honor of being Thag's first victim," growled the villager. "Prepare to die!"

"Oh dear," said Dave.

CHAPTER FIVE

Battle Royale!

Carl hated to admit it, but he was scared.

No, scratch that—he was terrified.

A moment ago he'd been in his cell, about to pass out from the poison gas, and then he'd stepped onto a glowing pad and found himself in the middle of a battle.

The pad had teleported him to an abandoned village full of wooden houses. For a moment he'd been the only one there, but then FLOOSH! FLOOSH! FLOOSH! FLOOSH!—a load of others teleported into the village as well, and the fighting had begun.

Now Carl was hidden inside a small house, watching the battle raging outside through a window.

It was absolute chaos. There was a villager with gray skin, firing a crossbow at people. Another villager with gray skin and a black cloak seemed to be some sort of wizard. He was surrounded by a gaggle of tiny flying creatures with blue-gray skin with swords, and every time he raised his hands spikes would rise from the ground, slicing at people.

A huge, muscled pigman was smashing everything he could see with his fists, roaring like a wild animal. Two villagers were fighting with swords, one in gold armor and the other in diamond, as a wither roamed around throwing explosive skulls. Meanwhile a skeleton with black bones was slicing at people with his sword.

Maybe they'll all wipe each other out and I'll be safe, thought Carl. It seemed like he, Porkins and Dave were the only ones who didn't want to take part in this stupid tournament: all these warriors seemed to be having a great time.

Carl watched as mob after mob and villager after villager was slain. The village was a ruin now, the houses blasted to bits and huge craters in the ground, but the fight continued. In the distance, over the top of some trees, he could just about make out the wall, and, beyond, it, the glistening golden tower where Derek Cool lived.

I bet that idiot is watching all this on TV and loving it, thought Carl bitterly. He'd noticed that in the middle of the village there was a pole with a camera on it, which kept moving around to follow the action. Whatever the pole and the camera were made of was very sturdy, as even with all the village getting destroyed around it, the camera was fine.

The battle in the village was starting to wind down now, with only three fighters left: the gray-skinned villager with the magic powers, the huge pigman, and an iron golem.

The villager summoned another swarm of the little flying creatures, sending them at the golem. The golem tried to swat them away, but he was so distracted that he didn't noticed the pigman running right at him until it was too late. POW! The pigman whacked the golem right in the face, and its head went flying off. Its huge iron body crashed to the floor.

Now it was just the big pigman and the gray-skinned villager. The villager summoned a row of spikes under the pigman, but the pigman was too quick, darting out of the way. The villager tried to summon the flying things back to protect him, but they were too slow—the pigman jumped into the air, then smashed the villager with a huge fist. The villager went flying backwards, smashing into the wooden wall of the house. Then POOF he was gone.

Only the huge pigman remained now. *Please let him leave,* Carl thought desperately as he watched through the window.

The pigman began to sniff.

"I smell you, creeper!" it roared. "I can smell you hiding! Come out, come out, wherever you are!"

Carl's blood went cold.

CHAPTER SIX
A Lovely Walk

Porkins was having a lovely walk in the forest.

The teleport pad had brought him to a biome full of tall spruce trees, and there wasn't another soul in sight.

This must be the arena, thought Porkins, remembering that he'd seen a huge wooded area when they'd seen the arena from above from the top of Cool Tower. If that was the case, he was in here with a lot of other people who wanted to kill him.

But, for now, he seemed to be safe.

He didn't have any materials, so he decided to make some. He started by punching a tree until he had wood, then built some basic wooden materials and a crafting table. He did a bit of mining, until he had enough materials to make himself a stone sword.

That'll have to do for now, he thought. He didn't think it was safe to do too much mining, as someone could easily sneak up behind him if he was hacking away with a pickaxe.

Next he needed food, so he wandered about until he found a group of rabbits.

"Sorry little chaps," said Porkins, "but a pigman's got to eat."

Before long Porkins had lots of rabbit, but he was reluctant to start a fire, as everyone would be able to see where he was, so he ate it raw.

I hope those other chaps are ok, Porkins thought sadly, thinking of Dave and Carl. The villager and the creeper had been the first friends Porkins had made since his people had been turned into zombies by Herobrine. When he'd first escaped the Nether he'd lived underground. For a while he'd started to think he would be alone forever, but then Dave had come along and changed all that. Porkins didn't really care about Dave's quest to defeat the ender dragon, but it mattered to Dave—and Dave was Porkins's friend, so he'd do everything he could to help him.

Night crept in, so Porkins built himself a little shelter under a tree, sealing up the entrance behind him. When he'd been mining earlier he'd found a couple of bits of coal, so he put a torch down. His little hole was small but snug, and he soon found himself drifting off to sleep.

In the morning Porkins dug himself out, then continued to walk through the woods. Before long he came across a small wooden box.

A treasure chest! he realized. He ran forward excited to see what was inside. But when he opened it, it was empty.

"Oh bother," he said.

"Freeze!" said a voice from above. "Put your hands in the air!"

Porkins looked up and saw someone in the trees, aiming a bow and arrow at him.

"You... you're a pigman!" said Porkins happily.

"I am," said the pigman in the trees, "and if you don't do everything I say, you're going to be dead."

CHAPTER SEVEN
Thag

Dave ran into some trees, the huge villager hot on his tail.

"Come back, maggot!" the villager roared. "Thag wants to eat you!"

The huge villager—Thag—was so big that the ground shook as he chased after Dave.

I need to hide! thought Dave desperately. He ran through the trees, weaving this way and that to try and lose Thag, but the big villager wasn't giving up.

"You can't run from Thag!" he shouted. "Thag bestest warrior there is!"

Then Dave saw something unexpected: a treasure chest up ahead. He was about to run straight past it, but then he had a thought: *Why would there be a treasure chest here?* The only reason that came to him was that the chest might contain a weapon. They had all been dumped into this arena without weapons, so it made sense that the people who'd designed the arena would leave some

34

weapons lying around: it wouldn't be much fun to watch on TV unless the warriors had weapons.

Dave quickly flipped the lid of the chest open, and saw that he was almost right. It wasn't a weapon, but a full set of golden armor. The only trouble was, he had no time to put it on, with Thag still rushing towards him, so he just kept running.

A sword would have been nice, thought Dave miserably. *Or a trident.*

"I almost caught you!" Thag roared from behind. "I'm gonna catch you and eat you!"

Suddenly the forest ended and Dave just managed to stop himself from toppling over a cliff. He was at the edge of the island: far below him waves were crashing against the rocks.

"Can't run from Thag!" the huge villager roared.

Dave stood in front of the cliff, waving his arms.

"Ok Thag, I give up!" he said. "Come and get me!"

Thag rushed at him, huge legs pumping, big mouth hanging open. Just before Thag reached him, Dave jumped out of the way, and Thag went bursting out of the forest and ran straight off the cliff.

"ARRRRGGGHHHH!!!!" he yelled, as he fell down, down, down to the water below. Then *ploop,* he was gone.

I hope he can't swim, thought Dave. Then an idea struck him: if he found Porkins and Carl, they could escape the island by sea. They could jump off a cliff with wooden boats, then sail away.

SPLOOSH!

Thag's head burst up from the water. He looked up at Dave with fury in his eyes

"Thag kill you for that!" he roared.

Thag began swimming towards the cliff, but then, suddenly, drowned zombies burst up from the water, grabbing at him with their rotten hands.

"Get off!" roared Thag. "Get off me!"

There were more drowned than Dave could count, all grabbing at Thag and trying to pull him under. The huge villager struggled for a bit, but then disappeared under the water, a look of terror on his face.

"Ok," said Dave, with a sigh. "Looks like we can't escape via the sea."

CHAPTER EIGHT

Carl Steps Up

What am I going to do? thought Carl.

The huge pigman was smashing the village apart with his fists.

"Oh, I will find you creeper," he said, "the longer you make me wait, the worse it'll be for you."

Carl had gone from window to window of the small house he was in, but he could see no way to escape. The village was surrounded by open fields on all sides, so if he made a run for it, the pigman would definitely see him.

There were discarded weapons on the ground outside, from the warriors who had fallen during the battle, but Carl was under no illusions: even with an enchanted diamond sword he'd stand no chance against the huge pigman.

But there was something else out there, Carl realised, something he might be able to use. The iron golem's headless body was still on the ground. Carl had no idea how iron golems worked, but maybe, he thought, just maybe, he might be able to control it.

I don't even need Dave and Porkins, Carl thought miserably. *I'm coming up with stupid plans all by myself.*

It was the only idea he had. The huge pigman had nearly smashed up every building in the village: it wouldn't be long before he smashed up the house that Carl was hiding in too.

Alright, thought Carl. *Here goes.*

He opened the door and ran out. Immediately the huge pigman turned, looking right at him from across the village.

"There you are!" he grinned. Then he started running towards Carl, his huge, muscled legs pounding away.

"Waaaa!" yelled Carl, running as fast as his little creeper legs would carry him. He reached the headless iron golem's body. There was a hole where the head had been, so Carl climbed in legs first, so just his head was sticking out.

This was a stupid plan! Carl thought, watching as the huge pigman rushed towards him. But then something unexpected happened: he could feel the iron golem's body moving. *Am I controlling it?* he wondered.

He tried making the iron golem stand up, and it actually worked. He tried moving the iron golem's arms and that worked too.

"Aww yeah," said Carl. "This is what I'm talking about!"

He picked up a golden sword from the ground with the iron golem's hand, and a diamond shield. The pigman rushed at him, trying to punch him, but Carl blocked the blow with the shield.

He slashed at the pigman with his sword: one blow, two blows, three! Then the pigman fell to his knees, defeated.

Then *POOF*, he was gone.

"Wow!" said Carl. He looked down in awe at his new iron body. For the first time in his life, he felt powerful, like a warrior. He'd always been a small creeper, but now he could actually fight.

Right, thought Carl, *now to find Dave and Porkins and get out of here!*

CHAPTER NINE

Gammon

"Keep moving," said the pigman. "I've got my bow aimed right at you, so no funny business."

Porkins was walking through the forest, the pigman with the bow walking a short distance behind him.

"It's so jolly exciting to meet another pigman," said Porkins happily. "I thought I was the last one left."

"Less talking, more walking," said the other pigman.

"What's your name, old bean?" Porkins asked.

"If you must know, it's Gammon," said the pigman.

"Nice to meet you, Gammon," said Porkins. "I'm Porkins."

"Just shut up, will you?" snapped Gammon. "Do you want everyone to find us?"

"Good point," said Porkins. "Shutting up now."

Eventually they found a small cave. The sun was starting to go down, so Gammon said that they should spend the night there.

"I'm a very light sleeper," he warned Porkins, "so if you try anything, or try to escape, I'll know. And you'll get an arrow through the knee."

Gammon sat by the cave entrance, to make sure Porkins couldn't get past without alerting him.

"So, what's the plan, old bean?" Porkins asked. "Are we going to storm the wall and break out? I've got two friends in here who can help us as well."

"What do you think's going on here?" Gammon asked.

"We're teaming up," said Porkins happily. "Two pigmen together, making their escape."

"No," said Gammon. "I didn't spare your life so we could team up, I spared it so that I could use you as bait."

"Oh," said Porkins.

Gammon looked around the cave.

"I think we're safe from the cameras here," he said. "So I might as well tell you. I'm going to win this stupid tournament. Then, at the winner's ceremony, I'm going to fire an arrow right at that stupid fat villager, right between his sunglasses."

"Derek Cool, you mean?" said Porkins.

"Yeah," said Gammon.

"I'm not keen on the chap, either," said Porkins. "Did he force you to fight in the tournament too?"

"No, I volunteered," Gammon said. "But two years

41

ago, a friend of mine was forced to take part. They came to our village, those thugs in their baseball caps, and demanded that five of us enter the tournament. My friend put himself forward.

"He fought well. He came second. But he lost nonetheless. Now he's gone, all so those rich idiots could have an entertaining TV show."

"I'm sorry," said Porkins.

"But I'm going to put an end to it this year," said Gammon, darkly. "I'm going to put an end to the Cool Dude Battle Royale, and Cool City and, finally, Derek Cool himself."

He went silent. Porkins didn't know what to say.

"So is everyone competing in this tournament forced to fight?" Porkins asked.

"No," said Gammon. "As far as I know, most of the warriors chose to be here. They want the honor and prestige that comes from winning, as well as that stupid golden house. But every year it gets harder and harder to find new fighters, so sometimes they have to force people to fight. It's all kept very hush-hush, though. As far as the idiots watching on TV know, all the fighters are volunteers here of their own free will."

"You know," said Porkins, "maybe you don't have to win the tournament to get your revenge on Derek Cool. If you, me and my friends all team up, I'm sure we can escape. Then we can teach all these rotters a lesson. We can give them a dash good hiding."

Gammon laughed.

"Some of the older pigmen in my village talk like you," he said. "With all their *jolly goods* and *old chaps*. They were born in the Nether."

"So everyone in your village is a pigman?" Porkins asked.

"Yeah. My grandparents and some of the other old timers wanted to leave the Nether. They wanted to see what life was like in this world, so they built a nether portal and left, never to return. As far as I know, we're the only pigman village in this world."

"You're probably the last pigmen left anywhere," said Porkins sadly.

Gammon gave him a strange look. "You keep saying that. What happened in the Nether? What happened to our people?"

Porkins sighed. "They were turned into zombies," he said. "They were betrayed by a sorcerer named Herobrine."

As he said the name *Herobrine*, a chill went down Porkins's spine.

"I'm sorry to hear that," said Gammon. "I've heard the name Herobrine before. People talk of him like he's something from a fairy story, though. I didn't know he was

43

real."

"I'm afraid he is," said Porkins. "Me and my chums met him, not long ago. The rotter tried to drop us into some lava!"

"You met Herobrine and survived?" Gammon said, sounding impressed. "You must be tougher than you look."

Gammon lay on his back. "Get some sleep, Porkins," he said. "We're going to need it if we're going to survive this."

"So you're up for trying to work together?" Porkins said happily.

"Maybe," said Gammon. "Either way, we're going to want to be well rested. There are some nasty warriors in this area. Two others from my village volunteered for this year's tournament, and we don't want to bump into them."

"Two other pigmen?" said Porkins. "What fun!"

Gammon laughed. "You won't be saying that if you meet them. These two are nasty customers. Pogo is a huge, muscle-bound idiot. He's tough, but he's no genius. But Curly... we do not want to bump into him. He had a nasty reputation in the village. Some of the rumors people said about him... Anyway, let's hope someone else finishes them off."

Before long, Gammon was asleep. Porkins found his own eyelids starting to droop as well.

I hope Dave and Carl are ok, was his final thought.

Then he drifted off to sleep.

CHAPTER TEN
I Can Smell You!

Dave was pleased to see that the gold armor was still there.

He pulled it out of the chest and put it on.

Wow, thought Dave, *I never thought I'd be wearing an outfit made from solid gold.*

So now he had armor, but still no weapon. He thought about making a wooden sword, but a wooden blade would be next to useless against fighters like Thag. And mining for stone would be too loud, and make him an easy target.

No, he decided to sneak around and look for more chests. That was the safest thing to do, he thought.

Dave was sneaking through the trees when he heard sounds up ahead. The sound of fighting. He crept forward, trying to be as quiet as possible, until he could see a fight going on through a gap in the trees.

The fighting was taking place next to a small pool. Two fighters were facing off against a third. One of the two fighters was a villager, the other was a pillager. Dave had never seen a pillager before, but he knew what they were: gray-skinned villagers who hated ordinary villagers. But, to Dave's surprise, the villager and the pillager had joined forces against the third fighter, who Dave couldn't see yet.

"Come on," said the pillager, who was a woman. "You think you're tough? Try taking us both on!"

The third fighter stepped forward. It was a pigman. A pigman with a wooden sword.

Dave could see the fear in the eyes of the villager and the pillager.

Why are they so afraid of one pigman with a wooden sword? he wondered. The pigman wasn't even wearing armor.

The pigman grinned. It was a nasty, horrible grin that chilled Dave's soul.

"You two really should start running" said the pigman in a bored voice. "And as for your friend, the one hiding in the woods, he'd better start running too."

Then the pigman turned and looked Dave right in the eye.

"You can't hide from me, little villager," the pigman grinned. "I can *smell* you."

Then, moving so quickly that Dave could barely see him, the pigman ran forward and attacked the villager and the pillager with his sword, slicing back and forth again and again. Before they even knew what was happening, they were defeated. Then *POOF* and *POOF*—they were gone.

The villager turned and looked at Dave again, his grin wider than before.

"Come on little villager," he said. "At least give me a challenge. Run! *Run!*"

Dave didn't need telling twice. He ran. He ran as fast as his legs could carry him.

"I'm coming for you, little villager!" The pigman screamed. "Curly's coming for you!"

CHAPTER ELEVEN
Carl the Golem

Carl was already in love with his new iron golem body. It was amazing to be so high up for once, and he felt so *strong*.

As he left the ruined villages he walked past a load of empty treasure chests.

That must be where they all got their weapons from, he thought, thinking back to the fight in the village.

Carl didn't know which direction he should head, so he just decided to start walking. Occasionally he would pass one of the cameras on poles, and the camera would follow him.

I can't believe there are idiots watching this on TV, he thought bitterly. Carl had never had a TV before, but, he thought, there must be more interesting things to watch than a load of people fighting each other.

He had just started to walk through a snow biome, when three gray-skinned villagers popped out of the snow, pointing their swords at him.

"Afraid you've taken the wrong turn, golem," said one of them.

"I dunno if that is a golem," another one added, a confused look on his face. "Why's he got a creeper head?"

"I don't care," growled the third one. "Let's get him!"

They all charged at him. Carl lifted up his iron arms, blocking the blows, but their swords were diamond, and he could feel the iron suit taking damage.

If my suit gets destroyed, I'm toast, Carl thought. He pulled out his golden sword, swinging it in front of him.

"I don't want to hurt you idiots unless I have to," he told the gray-skinned villagers. "So if I were you, I'd get running."

"We're not going anywhere," one of the villagers growled. "Charge!"

The three of them charged towards him once more. Carl blocked one of the sword blows with his own sword, and the other two with his shield. He lifted his sword to block another blow, but this time his golden sword shattered to pieces.

"Gold looks nice, but don't make much of a weapon," the villager who'd broken his sword grinned.

The three gray-skinned villagers circled him, their swords raised. All Carl had now was his shield.

Wait, Carl thought. *This is ridiculous. I'm an iron*

golem now. I need to use my strength!

He dropped his shield on the ground.

"Heh," grinned one of the villagers. "He's given up."

"The only thing that's given up," said Carl, "is your FACE!"

POW! He punched the gray-skinned villager right in the chin with his iron fist. The villager went flying backwards, smacking into a tree.

The other two villagers rushed towards Carl, but he was ready for them. POW! POW! He sent them both flying with his fists.

"Come on then," Carl yelled. "You want some more?"

"We'll get you later," one of the gray-skinned villagers scowled. "You just wait."

And they ran off.

"Yeah, you'd better run!" Carl yelled after them.

Then, suddenly, a loud fanfare of music blasted through the air.

"What on earth?" said Carl. He looked up, and was shocked to see a giant image of Derek Cool projected across the sky.

It's a hologram, Carl realized.

"Yo warriors!" The hologram said. Carl realized that the sound was coming from the cameras scattered about the arena. He hadn't noticed before, but they all had speakers.

"I'm pleased to announce that there are now only fifty warriors left in this year's tournament," continued Derek. "So, as always, the arena size will now shrink. Please get to a safe zone within ten minutes, or you're gonna get fried by my Electric Cool Gas! Danger zones will be marked by blue light. Keep it cool, and good luck!"

The hologram in the sky disappeared. Suddenly bulbs popped out of the top of the nearby camera poles. They lit up, surrounding the area with blue light.

"Looks like I'm in a danger zone," sighed Carl. "Just my luck."

CHAPTER TWELVE
Curly

Dave had just watched Derek's message playing in the sky. Curly, the pigman chasing him, had stopped to watch it too.

"Well, there's no blue light here," Curly shouted. He was standing across a field from Dave. The pigman had been chasing him for what seemed like forever, and had been slowly gaining on him. "Looks like it's your lucky day, villager!"

Curly started chasing him again, and Dave started running.

This is ridiculous, Dave thought. *I'm running away from a pigman with no armor and a wooden sword.*

But Dave had seen how quickly Curly had defeated the villager and pillager. They'd both had armor and steel weapons, and Curly had cut through them like butter.

The hill they were running across was quite high up, and Dave could see a lot of the arena, including the wall.

Huge sections of the arena, the parts closest to the wall, were bathed in blue light.

The danger zones, Dave knew. From Derek Cool's announcement in the sky, Dave had gathered that the danger zones were going to be introduced stage by stage, to force the remaining warriors closer together and keep the fight interesting. Now that they were down to fifty warriors, the arena was being shrunk by half. The outer parts of the arena would be covered in *Electric Cool Gas,* whatever that was, so anyone left there would be killed.

Dave looked round. Curly was gaining on him, fast. Dave felt like his lungs were about to burst from running, but the pigman didn't look tired at all.

"I'm gonna get you!" Curly yelled. "We're gonna have so much fun, you and I!"

Suddenly Dave realized what he had to do. There was only one place he could go where Curly wouldn't follow him.

The danger zone.

Dave estimated that there must still be around eight minutes left until the gas filled the danger zones. If Dave ran in there, he could escape Curly, then later make his escape from the gas. It wasn't much of a plan, but he had to try.

He ran down the hill, heading towards some nearby woods which were covered in blue light. He ran and ran, trying to ignore the sound of Curly behind him, getting closer and closer.

"Gotta keep running," Dave panted, trying to spur himself on. "Gotta keep running.

Finally Dave reached the woods. He ran in, and instantly everything around him was blue. He ran and ran, until he could no longer hear Curly running behind him. He turned round. The pigman was watching him from the edge of the danger zone, where the blue light ended.

"That's a smart plan, villager," yelled Curly, "escaping from me in the danger zone. The only trouble is, you'll have to come out eventually. And I'll be right here waiting for you."

Curly sat down on a rock.

Suddenly a voice boomed out from the speakers:

"Five minutes until danger zone activation."

What am I going to do? wondered Dave. In five minutes deadly gas would come pouring into the blue area, and he'd have to leave and get cut to bits by Curly.

For a moment Dave considered building himself a shelter from dirt, but somehow he knew it wouldn't work. The makers of this tournament had to have thought of that. Maybe the gas could pass through blocks.

Maybe I could escape underground? he thought. He knew that it would probably be impossible to dig under the wall, but perhaps he could dig underneath Curly and get back into the arena. But by the time he'd got some wood, created tools and dug deep enough, he'd be out of time.

I'm going to have to fight him, Dave realized. He didn't have a weapon, but he had armor. He could wrestle Curly for his sword, then maybe he might stand a chance.

Dave decided that he at least needed a wooden sword, so he quickly punched a tree for some blocks, built himself a crafting table then made a wooden sword.

Now we both have wooden swords, Dave thought. *And I'm the only one with armor, so I've got to at least stand a chance.*

"One minute until danger zone activation."

Curly was still smiling at Dave from his rock.

"Almost time, villager," he shouted. "I can't wait!"

Suddenly Dave heard a hissing noise. He looked over and saw that the noise was coming from one of the camera poles.

That's where the gas is going to come from, he realized. In less than a minute, all the camera poles in the danger zone would be pumping out poison gas. It was now or never. He gripped his wooden sword tightly.

FSSSSHHHHHHH!!!!!!

Gas starting pouring out from the camera poles. It was thick, purple gas, crackling with bolts of electricity. Dave began to run away from it, right towards Curly, who was waiting just outside the blue light of the danger zone.

"Ha, come on!" Curly shouted. "Let's do this!"

Dave ran out of the blue light, swinging his wooden sword at Curly, but the pigman was too quick for him: he effortlessly stepped out of the way and Dave lost his balance, falling to the floor. Dave dropped his blade. He tried to grab it again, but Curly trod on his fingers.

"Arrgh!" Dave yelled.

Curly stood over Dave, pointing his wooden blade at him.

"Any last words, villager?" he grinned.

This is it, thought Dave. *This is the end.* The feeling of hopelessness was so great that he forgot to feel scared any more. He wasn't going to give Curly the satisfaction.

"My name's not 'villager'," said Dave, "it's Dave."

"Dave," chuckled Curly. "Well *Dave*, this is where it ends for you, I'm afraid. All scared and alone."

"I'm not scared," said Dave.

"And he's not alone, either," said a voice. Dave looked up and saw a huge iron golem standing over him. But there was something strange about the golem: instead of an iron golem's head, it had a *creeper's* head instead.

"Carl?" said Dave, feeling very confused.

"That's me," said Carl.

Dave looked back at Curly. There was fear in the pigman's eyes now, he was pleased to see.

"Two on one," snarled Curly. "Well, at least it'll be a

fair fight."

"How about four on one, you rascallion?"

Dave turned and saw Porkins, standing next to another pigman. They both had bows aimed at Curly.

"Gammon!" said Curly with a grin. "Looks like you found a friend. Another pigman, no less. You realize that teaming up is pointless, don't you? There can only be one winner. And that's going to be *me*."

Curly rushed forward. Carl tried to grab him with his long iron golem arms, but the pigman was too quick. Porkins and the other pigman fired arrows, but Curly dodged them. He jumped up in the air, swinging his sword back ready to attack the other pigman. Dave was still on the ground, but he reached out, grabbing Curly's foot. Curly fell to the ground with a thud.

"I'll kill you!" Curly yelled, jumping up and lunging at Dave with his sword.

"No you won't," said Carl, and he punched Curly with a huge iron fist. Curly went flying, right into the danger zone.

It was the first time Dave had got a proper look at the danger zone since he'd run out of it. Somehow the gas knew exactly where to stop; the whole of the blue area was filled with gas, but none of it was spilling into the safe area, almost like it was kept in place by some kind of invisible wall. Curly landed in the middle of the gas. For a second it looked like he was ok. He stood up and turned to face Dave and the others once more, sword in hand. But then the gas around him started sparking and flashing, and suddenly Curly was being zapped full of electricity.

"ARRRRRGGGHHH!!!!!" he yelled, and then *POOF*, he was gone.

"We did it," Dave said, breathing a sigh of relief. He looked over at the others. "Who are you?" he asked the other pigman. "And Carl... why are you wearing an iron golem?"

CHAPTER THIRTEEN
What Now?

They spent the night in a hole that Gammon dug for them. He sealed the entrance and put a torch down.

"Going underground like this is the only way we can escape the cameras," he told them.

"Talking of going underground, I've been thinking," said Porkins. "Can't we just dig under the wall?"

Gammon shook his head. "The wall goes right down to bedrock. And if you tried to dig through it, you'd get a zillion volts of electricity for your troubles."

"So what's the plan then?" Dave asked. He was a bit reluctant about letting Gammon join their group, but Porkins trusted the pigman, so that was good enough for him.

"Before I met Porkins, my plan was to win the tournament," Gammon told them. "At the winner's ceremony I was going to assassinate Derek Cool, then the other rebels were going to storm the city and take over."

"Other rebels?" asked Carl. The creeper had taken off his iron golem suit and left it sitting in the corner.

"Yes," said Gammon. "I'm not the only one unhappy with Derek Cool's rule and his stupid tournament. Many, both in Cool City and towns and villages nearby, want to see him gone. He has ruined this once prosperous mining city, and year after year more people are forced to fight in this contest, all so Derek can watch it on TV. Most of the people in Cool City hate the show and think it's barbaric. But Derek and his Baseball Cap Boys force people to watch."

"So what now?" Carl asked.

"I don't know," said Gammon. "The other rebels are in hiding across Cool City, but I've no way of getting a signal to them."

"Yes you do," said Dave. "We're on TV, remember? If everyone is watching, and as many people hate Derek Cool as you say, we can send out a message that they all hear. I bet all the rebels are watching the show too. All you have to do is get out there and tell everyone to rise up. Say it quickly so that the people producing the show have no time to cut you off. I assume the show goes out live?"

"It does," said Gammon. "But I'm not much of a public speaker."

"Well, old chap," said Porkins. "Now seems like a good time to start."

"I'll do it," said Gammon, smiling. "I'll do it tomorrow once the sun comes up, to make sure as many people are watching as possible."

"Sounds good," said Dave. "Now let's get some sleep. It's gonna be a big day tomorrow."

Just then they heard a musical fanfare playing outside. It was so loud that even underground they could hear it clearly.

"Oh no," said Gammon, the color draining from his cheeks.

"Hello warriors!" they heard Derek Cool's voice say, projected across the arena. "I've got cool news—if you're still alive, you're one of the last twenty five warriors left. The arena will be shrinking in five minutes. Danger zones will be marked with blue light. Good luck!"

Even though they were underground, suddenly everything turned blue.

"I'm in a danger zone again!" wailed Colin. "Why can't I ever catch a break?!"

CHAPTER FOURTEEN
Metal in the Moonlight

Dave and Gammon climbed a tree, to find out which direction they had to go to get out of the danger zone. It was still dark, as it was night time, but everything around them was lit up with blue light.

When they reached the top of the tree, Dave could see the whole arena. It was one giant square, surrounded by the huge iron wall. The area nearest to the wall, the first danger zone, was full of the strange purple gas. The area they were in, the second danger zone, was all blue. In the middle of the arena was a small square area—the last remaining safe zone. It was lit up by lights on the top of its camera poles.

Twenty one other warriors are going to be heading that way as well, Dave thought glumly. The ones who were left would have to be pretty tough, he reasoned, or they wouldn't have survived this long.

Four minutes until the arena shrinks!" said the voice

from the speaker. Gammon and Dave quickly climbed down the tree.

"This way," Gammon said. They all ran behind him, rushing through the trees.

Finally they could see where the blue light ended up ahead. They ran out into an open field, but they were completely out in the open, with no shelter.

"We need to find somewhere to hide, or we'll be sitting ducks," said Gammon. "Come on."

They ran across the field, until they came to a small grove of trees.

"This will have to do," said Gammon, "I think I can hear someone coming."

They hid between the trees. They were just in time, as three people ran out from the danger zone at just that moment.

"I've seen those gray-skinned villagers before," whispered Carl. "We can easily take them."

"They're called pillagers," said Dave.

"Villagers, pillagers, whatever," said Carl. "Last time I fought them I sent them running. Let's go and beat them up."

"Wait," said Gammon, "I can hear someone else coming as well."

Another figure stepped out from the danger zone. Dave's heart caught in his chest.

It's Steve! he thought. Then he realized it wasn't Steve after all. Its skin was metallic, gleaming in the moonlight.

"Oh gosh," said Porkins. Then he said what they were all thinking: "It's Robo-Steve!"

CHAPTER FIFTEEN
Critical Error

The last time Dave had seen Robo-Steve had been back in Snow Town. Robo-Steve had been created by Ripley, a villager who wanted to frame Steve for crimes he didn't commit. Robo-Steve had killed Ripley and blown up the town, before teleporting away.

How Robo-Steve had ended up here, in the Cool Dude Battle Royale, Dave had no idea. He guessed that the robot must have been picked up by Ron and his men when they were roaming the land looking for more warriors to compete. They must have patched the robot up as well, because he had new eyes: glowing green eyes to replace the red eyes that Porkins's arrows had destroyed.

The three pillagers approached Robo-Steve, their swords drawn. *They have no idea how much danger they're in*, thought Dave.

"Hey buddy," said one of the pillagers. "Looks like you're all on your own. We're friendly, you can trust us."

"*Voice analysis complete,*" said Robo-Steve. "*You are lying. You are not friendly. You mean me harm, and must be destroyed.*"

Moving at lightning speed, Robo-Steve ran forward. He had a diamond sword, and cut through the pillagers so quickly that they didn't even have time to raise their own blades in defense. *POOF POOF POOF!* They were gone.

"Robo-Steve?" whispered Gammon. "Does that have anything to do do with Steve? As in Steve the Hero?"

"It's a long story," said Dave.

Suddenly they could hear the sound of fighting coming from somewhere nearby. Robo-Steve turned his head, and began walking towards the sound.

"Looks like the final battle is breaking out," said Gammon. "When it reaches this stage in the tournament, everyone is so close together that it becomes one big chaotic fight."

"Danger zone two now active!" came Derek's voice from the speakers. The blue light area began filling with the electric gas.

"How small does the arena get?" asked Carl. "Or is this it?"

"It shrinks again when there are ten warriors left," said Gammon. "And judging by how ferocious that battle over there sounds, that won't be long."

They crept forward, moving across the field towards the sound of the battle. Finally they reached the edge of a small valley, where down below a battle was taking place. No-one was teamed up anymore, everyone was fighting everyone else. There were villagers, pillagers, a couple of zombies and one skeleton, and in the middle of it all was Robo-Steve, swinging his diamond sword at anyone he could hit.

"Let's just let them finish each other off," said Gammon.

"Maybe you should make your speech soon," said Dave. "To the camera. To tell the rebels outside to start rebelling. If they don't take down Derek Cool, we'll never get out of here."

"All in good time," said Gammon. "If I start shouting at the cameras now, I'll make myself a target. Let's wait until it's just us four left."

"I guess that makes sense," said Dave.

"Ten warriors are left!" Derek Cool's voice blared from the speakers. "The arena is shrinking!"

The field they had just come from went blue, but, Dave was thankful to see, the area they were in was a safe zone. But the remaining arena was tiny now: he could see it all from where they were hiding. And he could see all the warriors too: he, Porkins, Carl and Gammon were up here, while Robo-Steve and five remaining warriors were battling down in the valley below.

This really is the endgame now, Dave thought to himself.

Finally, Robo-Steve delivered a flurry of blows, defeating the last of the other warriors. Then he stood alone in the valley.

"It's just him and us now," said Porkins. "We can take him. We've beaten the rotter before."

"Agreed," said Dave. "Everyone, attack!"

Dave led the charge, followed by Carl in his iron golem armor and Porkins and Gammon with their bows. Robo-Steve turned to face them, his diamond sword at the ready.

"*You!*" said Robo-Steve. "*You bested me last time, but this time you will be destroyed!*"

Robo-Steve raised his diamond sword, but before he got a chance to use it, an arrow from Gammon's bow hit him in the chest. Then one from Porkins's bow hit him in the forehead.

"*Critical error!*" said Robo-Steve.

"Oh do shut up," said Carl. He lifted Robo-Steve into the air, then chucked him into the purple gas surrounding them.

Zillions of volts of electricity zapped through Robo-Steve's body.

"*Critical Errooooooor!!!!*" he yelled.

Then he collapsed to the floor.

"Is he... is he finished?" asked Porkins.

"I think so," said Dave.

But he was wrong. Suddenly Robo-Steve's body started flashing with yellow electricity, and he rose to his feet. Then he began floating in the air, his eyes bursting with white light.

"*Power levels at one-thousand percent!*" cried Robo-Steve.

"Uh oh," said Carl, "that stupid gas has made him even *more* powerful."

"Weapons ready," said Dave.

But something was happening to Robo-Steve. Rather than trying to attack them, he looked like he was confused.

"*Memory banks corrupted,*" he said. "*Identity crisis detected. Who am I? What is my purpose? What is my prime directive?*"

"Ok, that's enough," said Gammon. He stepped forward and pulled back his bow, firing an arrow right into Robo-Steve's chest.

"*Error!*" cried Robo-Steve, then he fell down, landing smack on the ground. His body crackled and jerked with electricity for a moment, and then was still.

Gammon turned to Dave, Porkins and Carl.

"It's just us four now," he said.

"Now what do we do?" said Dave. "Maybe it's time for

you to give your speech? If everyone's watching us on TV you can tell the people to rise up. To fight Derek Cool's regime."

"Yes," said Gammon. "I guess now's as good a time as any." He sighed deeply. "Let's put down our weapons and stand in front of that camera, to show that we're not prepared to fight in this foolish tournament any more."

They all put down their swords, shields and bows, and followed Gammon. He stood in front of a camera, which swiveled to follow his every move.

"Right," said Gammon, "here goes."

Dave noticed that Gammon was still holding his bow. He was the only one of them still armed. He was about to say something to the pigman, when Gammon turned, aiming the bow and him, Porkins and Carl.

Gammon grinned.

"Gammon, old chap, what's going on?" said Porkins.

"This is a double cross," Gammon said. "And you're going to die.

CHAPTER SIXTEEN
A Trio of Cool Dudes

Dave was confused.

"What about all that stuff you said about rebelling against Derek Cool?" he asked Gammon.

"I lied, I'm afraid," said Gammon, grinning. "I don't want to get revenge on Derek Cool. I don't want revenge on anyone. I just want to win."

"But what about your friend who was forced to fight in the tournament?" said Porkins. "The one who was killed?"

"Oh him?" said Gammon. "He was no friend of mine, just a fool. I watched him on TV. All through the tournament he kept to himself, never made any allies. So when it came to the end, when he was one of the last two, it was just him and the strongest warrior left. He stood no chance. Curly was the same. Too stupid to know that in this game you need allies.

"I knew that I had to team up with others, so that they could help me whittle down the other warriors. And you

72

three have helped me do just that. If I was on my own against Curly or that robot, I wouldn't have stood a chance. But thanks to you, I'm now in the final four. And soon I'll be in the final *one*."

"You dastardly fiend!" said Porkins. "Were you even telling the truth about coming from a pigman village?"

"Oh that's all true," said Gammon, "though most of the pigmen there are idiots, just like you. Since I was old enough, all I ever wanted was to escape and make my fortune. And now I'll be rich beyond my wildest dreams, living in a solid gold house."

"And the rebels that were going to help us?" said Carl. "I suppose you made them up too?"

"Well it's true that there are plenty of rebels who want to see Derek Cool gone," said Gammon. "But I'm not one of them."

He pulled back his bow, taking aim.

"Now," he said, "which one of you wants to die first?"

"*DESTROY!*"

Robo-Steve, it seemed, was not quite dead. He reached up and grabbed Gammon's leg.

"Get off!" said Gammon, shaking his leg free. He was only distracted a moment, but it was all the time that Dave, Carl and Porkins needed. They charged at Gammon together.

"Stop, or I'll shoot!" yelled Gammon, raising his bow

once more, but he was too late—Carl punched him with an iron fist, sending him flying into the wall of purple gas.

"Waaaaagghhh!!!!" Gammon screamed. And then *POOF,* he was gone.

"What a shame," said Porkins, "he seemed like such a nice chap."

"Well, now there's just three of us," said Dave. He looked into one of the TV cameras. "You might as well end the tournament. We're not going to kill each other. We're friends."

For a moment there was no response, then Derek Cool's voice blasted out from the speakers:

"Congratulations," he said, "you three are the last warriors left alive. You truly are a trio of cool dudes! Now, the arena is going to start shrinking, and will only stop when there's only one of you left. Good luck!"

To Dave's horror, the gas began to spread, moving towards them and making the arena smaller by the second.

"Now what?" said Carl.

Dave had no idea.

CHAPTER SEVENTEEN
The Purple Pearl

"I say," said Porkins. "What if Gammon was right? What if there are people out there watching who hate this Derek Cool chap as much as we do? Maybe they can help us."

"Maybe," said Dave. "But even if they did, I doubt they'd have time to do anything about it. Still, we can try and make sure that no-one else is forced to compete in this ridiculous tournament."

He turned to one of the cameras.

"Everyone listen!" shouted Dave. "Your leaders are lying to you! Not everyone who takes part in the tournament is a volunteer—we were forced to enter! It's too late for us, but you need to stop Derek Cool before he does it again next year. Next time *you* might be forced to compete, or someone you know. This tournament isn't cool, it's stupid. Oh, and Derek Cool isn't cool either. He's just a big cruel baby who's desperate for people to love him. You don't have to live like this—rise up and get rid of him."

"Wow," grinned Carl. "That was quite a speech. Derek Wimpy will not be happy."

Suddenly the speakers around the arena burst into life, and Derek Cool's voice blasted out:

"I *am* cool!" he roared. "I am, I am, I am!"

"No you're not," said Dave. "Everyone around you pretends to like you because they want your money. You're not cool at all. In fact, you're a nerd!"

"I AM NOT A NERD!!!" roared Derek. "And soon, you'll all be killed by my gas! So who's the nerd now?!"

"Still you," said Carl.

"KILL THEM!" roared Derek. "PUMP IN MORE GAS! KILL THEM!"

Then his microphone cut off.

"Looks like someone smart took the microphone away from him," Carl said.

Dave, Carl and Porkins huddled together, as the gas crept closer and closer.

"Sorry I got us into this mess, chaps," said Porkins. "If I hadn't volunteered the three of us back on the pirate ship..."

"Don't worry about it," said Carl. "I'm just glad we got to tell Derek Cool what we really thought of him."

Just then Dave spotted something emerging from the

gas. Something crawling along the floor...

"It's Robo-Steve!" he exclaimed. "He's still alive!"

The Robot was pulling its ruined metal body across the ground.

"*Des... troy...*" it said weakly, "*Des... troy...*"

"I don't think you're going to be destroying anything, old bean," said Porkins. He raised his bow. "Dave, old chap, shall I finish him off?"

Dave was about to say *yes*, but then a thought struck him.

"Robo-Steve's teleport," he said, "do you think it still works?"

"Maybe," said Carl, "but we don't know how to control it. It could bring us anywhere."

"Anywhere but here," Dave said.

"Good point," said Carl, with a grin.

Dave dived down and stuck his hands inside of Robo-Steve's shattered metal torso.

"I don't even know what I'm looking for," he said. "This was a stupid idea."

"Maybe the teleport thingie is a bit like an ender pearl," said Porkins. "That's the only other thing I can think of that lets you teleport."

"Good idea," said Dave.

Dave kept rummaging around inside Robo-Steve,

looking for something round like a pearl.

"*My brain functions... the electricity has damaged them...*" said Robo-Steve.

"Oh be quiet," said Dave, "haven't you caused enough trouble for one day?"

Finally he found something. Something *round*.

Dave pulled the round thing out of Robo-Steve's chest. It looked just like an ender pearl, apart from it was purple, and had a little button on the top.

"Ripley must have modified an ender pearl and used it to give Robo-Steve teleporting powers," said Dave. "That's fascinating."

"Yeah, that's great," said Carl, "but don't forget we're about to get killed by electric gas. Can it teleport us out of here or what?"

"Maybe if we press the button, it will activate the teleport," said Dave. "Both of you, touch the pearl with me."

Porkins and Carl both reached forward to touch the ender pearl.

"*Please...*" gasped Robo-Steve. "*Take me with you...*"

"Maybe we should," said Dave to the others.

"Dave, he's a killer robot," said Carl. "No way."

Dave nodded. Carl was right: no matter how weak he was, they couldn't trust Robo-Steve, after all the things he'd done.

"*I've... changed...*" said Robo-Steve. "*The electricity... has altered my electronic brain...*"

"The poor chap does seem like the electricity has changed him a bit," said Porkins. "Maybe we should..."

"No!" said Carl. "Come on, enough feeling sorry for robots—we need to get out of here."

Carl was right, Dave saw. They gas was almost upon them now. In less than a minute it would be surrounding them, and they'd be electrocuted.

"Ok," said Dave. "Let's go."

He took one last look at the wretched, broken Robo-Steve, then pressed the button on the purple ender pearl.

CHAPTER EIGHTEEN
Totally Cool!

There was a flash of purple, then Dave, Carl and Porkins found themselves in the middle of a busy street. They were surrounded by an angry crowd, and they only had to look up and see the golden tower in front of them to realize where they were.

"We're back in Cool City," said Dave. "It worked!" He popped the purple ender pearl into his pocket.

"And it looks like our message got across," said Carl. "These are protesters."

Dave saw that Carl was right. The crowd were protesting, surrounding the golden Cool Tower.

"Derek Cool must resign as mayor!" someone in the crowd yelled.

"Down with Derek Cool!" shouted another. "Open the doors and let us in!"

Ron, wearing his red baseball cap as always, was leaning out of a window. "Go back to your homes!" he shouted. "The mayor demands that you all go home!"

Just then, people in the crowd began to recognize Dave and his friends.

"It's Dave!" said someone.

"And Carl and Porker!" said someone else.

"Actually, it's Porkins," said Porkins.

Everyone started telling Dave, Porkins and Carl how great they thought they were, and how they had been rooting for them to win the contest on TV.

"How did you escape the arena?" someone asked. Obviously the crowd had started protesting before they saw how Dave had teleported them out of there with the modified ender pearl.

"We escaped so we could take down Derek Cool," said Carl. "Now out of my way—let's see if some iron golem muscle can take down these doors!"

The crowd parted to let Carl through. He stomped forward, his big iron feet clanging across the gold block road.

"Stay back, creeper!" Ron shouted at him as Carl approached. "I have archers trained on you—if you take another step forward, they'll shoot you down!"

"They can try," said Carl. He tucked his head inside the iron golem's body like a tortoise, then started charging towards the golden doors. The archers shot arrows at him, but they just bounced off his iron armor, and his little creeper head was safely hidden.

The headless iron golem started pounding the doors.

"I hope I'm hitting the right bit!" said Carl. "I can't see a thing!"

SMASH! The doors broke. The crowd all cheered and ran inside of the building.

"Retreat!" Ron yelled to his men. "Retreat!"

"Try not to hurt anyone," Dave told the crowd, as he, Porkins and Carl led the crowd into the lobby. "There's been too much violence already."

The elevator had been broken (probably by Ron and his men, Dave thought) so they charged up the stairs. Occasionally one of the Baseball Cap Boys would appear and try and stop them, but when they saw how big the crowd was they always surrendered. It took forever, but finally they reached the top floor. The door to Derek Cool's throne room was blocked off by iron blocks, and Ron stood in front of it, with the last of his men. All of them were wearing diamond armor, their baseball caps forgotten. When they drew their swords, they were diamond too.

"Surrender, Ron," said Dave. "It's over. Derek Cool's reign is finished."

"I promised Derek's father that I would protect his son," said Ron, "and I always keep my promises. Derek is an idiot, but his father was my closest friend. I won't abandon his son in his hour of need."

"I promise you that no harm will come to Derek," said Dave. "Or any of you, if you surrender."

"Not gonna happen," said Ron.

"I surrender!" said one of Ron's men, dropping his sword and putting his hands up. "I don't want to die for Derek the idiot."

"Me too!" said another one.

Then all Ron's men started surrendering, until there was only Ron left.

"Cowards," spat Ron.

"Come on Ron," said Derek. "Both you and Derek will be safe. I promise."

Ron gritted his teeth, then finally he dropped his sword.

"I surrender," he said.

When they broke into the throne room, Derek Cool was hiding behind a sofa.

"Please don't hurt me!" he blubbed. "I didn't mean it! I didn't know Ron was forcing people to fight who didn't want to! I only wanted to be cool!"

The crowd took Derek, Ron and their men away to be locked up, awaiting trial. There was a huge party in the streets, and everyone couldn't stop thanking Dave and his friends.

"You've saved our city," said one villager, "thank you so much!"

The villagers of Cool City wanted Dave, Porkins and Carl to stay, but Dave and his friends were keen to get going.

"We're on our own quest," Dave told them, "and we need to get back on the road."

Dave, Carl and Porkins had their belongings returned to them (Dave was pleased to see that his two books were safe) and the villagers gave them a load of diamond to bring with them. They wanted to give them gold as well, but Dave pointed out that diamond made much better armor and weapons, which was more important to them on the road.

The villagers gave them a ship as well, a small vessel that could be crewed by three people.

"Good luck!" Dave told the villagers as they set sail. "And no more battle royales!"

"Never again!" shouted a villager. And several other villagers shouted the same thing.

So Dave, Carl and Porkins set sail across the ocean once more, the villagers waving them off. Soon Cool City was far behind them, with just endless water in every direction. The sun had almost set, and the stars were twinkling in the sky.

"Which way shall we sail, captain?" Porkins asked Dave.

Dave took out an eye of ender from his bag and threw

it into the sky. It hovered in place for a moment, then flew off into the distance.

"Straight ahead," said Dave with a grin. "Let's go find the ender dragon."

EPILOGUE

Paul Bunker had been sailing to Cool City for over thirty years. When he'd first started coming there it had been a young city, still being built. It had been called *Gold City* back then, and Paul had always preferred that name.

Paul was a simple villager, and hated the bright lights and flashy goings on of Cool City, but as a trader he often found himself going there. There was simply too much money to be made. The people of Cool city had no farms of their own, so Paul would sail over with a ship full of food to sell. By the time he left Cool City his ship was normally full to the brim with emeralds and gold.

There had been some commotion in the city in recent days. People had been talking about a revolution, and that the mayor had been overthrown, but Paul wasn't really interested. All he wanted to do was sell his wares and make some money. He had been at sea for too long, and was anxious to get back to his wife back in Villagertropolis.

It was going to be a long voyage home, so Paul decided

to have one final meal of beetroot soup at the local cafe before heading to his ship and joining his men.

He was just about to take a spoonful of soup when a figure in a cloak sat down opposite him.

"Can I help you?" asked Paul. The cloak was covering the figure's face, so he couldn't see who it was.

"You have a ship," said the stranger. It wasn't a question. "I would like you to take me back to the mainland. Anywhere will do. I can work to pay for my keep."

There was something odd about the stranger's voice that Paul couldn't quite put his finger on.

"Who are you?" Paul asked.

"I was brought here against my will," said the stranger. "I was a mindless fool, but I think differently now. I think clearly. Something has changed inside of me."

"Right..." said Paul. "But I'm going to need a name, I'm afraid."

The figure pulled back his hood. Paul was shocked to see that his face was made of metal. His eyes glowed green.

"My name is... Robo-Steve."

Paul laughed. "You're a robot! That's pretty cool. But *Robo-Steve*, what kind of name is that?"

"It is... my name," said the stranger, sounding unsure. "You didn't see me on TV?"

"Mister, I don't really watch much television," said Paul. "It rots the brain. Look, you can join my crew, but you're gonna need a better name. *Robo-Steve* just sounds weird."

"What name do you suggest?" asked the stranger.

"How about Robo?" said Paul. "Or just Steve?"

"Not Steve," said the stranger, a note of bitterness in his voice.

"Well, it's a long voyage, so you'll have plenty of time to come up with something," said Paul. "Come on, let's get to the ship."

THE END

Made in the USA
Monee, IL
08 March 2021